HORSE DIARIES
· Yatimah ·

HORSE DIARIES

HORSE DIARIES

Yatimah

CATHERINE HAPKA

illustrated by RUTH SANDERSON

RANDOM HOUSE NEW YORK

Text copyright © 2011 by Catherine Hapka
Illustrations copyright © 2011 by Ruth Sanderson
Photo credits: © Bob Langrish (p. 152); Library of Congress (pp. 147, 148–49, 151).

All rights reserved. Published in the United States by Random House Children's Books, a division of Random House, Inc., New York.

Random House and the colophon are registered trademarks of Random House, Inc.

Visit us on the Web! www.randomhouse.com/kids

Educators and librarians, for a variety of teaching tools, visit us at www.randomhouse.com/teachers

Library of Congress Cataloging-in-Publication Data
Hapka, Cathy.
Yatimah / Catherine Hapka ; illustrated by Ruth Sanderson. — 1st ed.
p.   cm. — (Horse diaries ; [6])
Summary: In a mid-ninth-century Bedouin camp in the Arabian Desert, a horse is born to a prized Arabian war mare who dies during the birth, and the foal is raised with dreams of continuing her mother's glory as a war mare. Includes facts about Arabian horses and their importance to Bedouin tribes.
ISBN 978-0-375-86719-4 (trade) — ISBN 978-0-375-96719-1 (lib. bdg.) — ISBN 978-0-375-89764-1 (ebook)
1. Arabian horse—Juvenile fiction. [1. Arabian horse—Fiction.
2. War horses—Fiction. 3. Horses—Fiction. 4. Bedouins—Fiction.
5. Middle East—History—9th century—Fiction.] I. Sanderson, Ruth, ill. II. Title.
PZ10.3.H2258Yat 2010   [Fic]—dc22   2009053906

Printed in the United States of America

10 9

First Edition

CONTENTS

"Oh! if people knew what a comfort to horses a light hand is . . ."
—from *Black Beauty*, by Anna Sewell

HORSE DIARIES
· Yatimah ·

A Bedouin Camp in the Arabian Desert, Ninth Century AD

My first memory was of human hands upon me, helping to pull me free of my mother's body. It was night, and a low moon hung round and pale in the clear dark sky. For a moment I lay there blinking upon the sand, not knowing who or what I was or what was happening.

"Praise Allah, the foal is alive," a human voice said as the hands left me.

"Never mind the foal," another voice called out from very close by. It belonged to a tall man with a bristly black beard and weather-beaten skin that told of many years beneath the desert sun. The harsh, anxious sound of his voice made my ears twitch, even though I didn't understand what the words meant. "Something is wrong. Sarab is bleeding too much!"

"Are you sure?" a third voice said. "It was a difficult foaling. . . ."

There was movement, fabric swishing past me as more humans came to bend over the mare lying still on the sand.

I blinked my eyes, swiveling my ears around. There was so much to see and hear that it was difficult to focus. The sky overhead was dark except for the bright moon and a dusting of stars. A breeze tickled the whiskers of my muzzle, and the air felt cool though the sand beneath my body was warm. Nearby stood a large tent made of camel hide, and I could smell and hear other animals moving around on the far side of a grove of palm trees. I wanted to react to all of it, but I didn't know what to do first.

Then a human girl kneeled down in front of me, blocking my view of all else. Her hands reached for me, stroking my face and neck. She had a light touch, like wind through an oasis, and her dark eyes were large and kind.

"It's a filly, Father," the girl called out in a voice filled with wonder. "She's perfect!"

"Keep her out of the way, Safiya." The older man's voice still sounded harsh. "Sarab is in trouble."

Safiya looked toward the mare. "Is she going to be all right?"

"I don't know. It is for Allah to decide now."

The girl stayed where she was, crouched over me. Her eyes turned back to mine, ignoring the commotion going on near the mare.

"It's all right, little one," she whispered, stroking the dampness out of my fuzzy foal coat. "Your mama is going to be all right. Allah wouldn't let anything happen to Father's favorite war mare."

I still didn't understand the words. But the

girl's voice sounded uncertain. That made me curious enough to stretch my long neck forward until I could snuffle her face, seeking the scent of her. The girl laughed and pushed my nose gently away.

Another man rushed past, younger than the others and with a lighter beard. Sand flew up from beneath his running feet and pinged against my hide. That made me raise my head and snort in surprise. The effort of doing so tipped me over onto my side.

But I quickly righted myself. That was when I noticed a pair of long legs folded beneath my body. Could they belong to me?

Oh yes! They twitched, and I suddenly understood what they were meant for. Lurching forward onto my sternum, I flung my forelegs out and then scrambled upward.

"Oh! She's trying to stand already!" Safiya exclaimed. She cried out as I swayed and fell back to the sand.

But I was already trying again. This time I remembered to organize my hind legs as well. A second later, I was standing!

I let out a nicker of triumph. The girl reached out to steady me as I stood swaying there, all four legs splayed in different directions. I leaned against her for a moment, grateful for the help.

The other humans weren't paying any attention to me. There were four or five of them, all bent over the horse still lying on the sand: my dam. Her sides were heaving, her black coat slick with sweat. I couldn't see much else of her. Then someone moved, his pale robes swirling

out of the way, and I finally saw my dam's face. She had a fine, chiseled head with a jagged blaze running down it. Her large eyes were rolling and staring. Her nostrils flared with each labored breath.

I knew I wanted to get closer to her. To do that, I had to figure out how to move. My legs trembled, seeming to know what to do. I took a wobbly step forward, nearly falling again.

"Keep her away!" one of the men barked out.

Young Safiya put gentle hands on my neck and shoulder. "Stay back, little one," she said. "They're trying to help your mama."

But there was to be no help for my dam. A few minutes later, her eyes closed. Her graceful neck went limp on the sand. And the tall, bearded man let out a heartbroken cry that echoed across the desert.

"I'm sorry, Father," one of the younger men said. "Sarab was a fine mare. But at least you still have her daughter."

"Yes." Another man stepped toward me for a closer look. "And look, Nasr, she has her dam's fine head and long legs. Sarab will live on in this one."

"That's right, Father," Safiya put in. "Isn't she beautiful?"

But her father, Nasr, did not turn toward me. "I do not wish to look upon the foal that took Sarab's life," he said, his voice shaking with emotion. "Find it a nurse mare and leave me alone."

He kneeled down beside Sarab's body as the

other humans exchanged glances. I understood none of what was happening, though I could sense that their faces and voices were troubled.

But I was troubled by something else. Hunger. Now that I was up and moving around, I felt my belly begin to grumble. Instinct told me that I needed to find food soon. But where?

I turned and nudged at Safiya, seeking any sign of something to fill my belly. She patted me and pushed me away, so I turned to the next closest human, one of the younger men. When I nosed at his robes, he glanced down at me.

"The filly needs milk," he said. "Shall we see if Jumanah will accept her?"

"That's a good idea," another said. "Jumanah is a strong, stout mare and always has plenty of milk. And her colt is only a few days old."

"Yes, the filly can share his mother, or have her all to herself for all I care," someone else added. "What need have we of another colt?"

"Hush, brother," the first man said. "All horses are gifts from Allah. We can use the colt as a pack animal when he's older, or use him for breeding if he is worthy, or perhaps trade him away for something we need. When last we parted from our cousin Rami and his family, they were complaining that several of their horses are getting too old to carry much weight during their moves. I'm sure they'd be glad to trade us a few sheep for a strong, stout, tall colt like that one."

The other man shrugged. "You're right, but this filly is much more valuable than any colt, especially if she grows up to be a great war mare like her dam." He shot a look toward Nasr, who was still bent over Sarab's body. "No matter what Father might think of her right now."

The first man hurried off into the darkness, returning moments later with two horses walking behind him. One was a foal not much older than I was, a tall chestnut colt. But I paid little attention to him. My nose twitched as I caught the scent of the other horse, a flea-bitten gray mare with a robust build and a calm expression.

I let out a cry of eagerness and leaped toward her, almost toppling over. Several strong hands caught me and guided me toward the mare, while one of the men took hold of the colt and kept him away, though he nickered and kept trying to get close enough to sniff at me.

The mare, Jumanah, didn't object as I found

the place to nurse. Soon I was drinking eagerly, my short tail flapping back and forth in time to my suckling. Jumanah turned and smelled me carefully, then nuzzled kindly at my flank.

"That's a relief," someone observed as the humans all watched me drink. "At least this little orphan will have a chance now with Jumanah looking after her."

"Don't call her an orphan," Safiya said with a frown.

"Why not?" the youngest of the men said with a shrug. I would later learn he was one of Safiya's brothers. "That's what she is, and there's no shame in it."

And so I had my name. From that moment onward, the humans referred to me as Yatimah, which means *orphan* in their language. Jumanah accepted me as her own; just as the humans had hoped, she had milk and attention enough for both me and her own colt, Tawil. And I was content with that, for I knew no different.

Two Months Old

*Y*atimah, *stand still!* Jumanah told me with a snort of exasperation.

I kicked up my heels and spun around to face the patient gray mare. The morning sun hadn't yet burned off the cool of the desert night, and a breeze lifted my tail and sent a lively shiver through my sturdy body.

I can't stand still! I told Jumanah. *There's too much to do. Hurry, Tawil, let's go wake up the goats!*

Tawil was nursing. But he looked up when I called to him, milk beading on his whiskers.

In a minute, Yatimah, he said. *I'm still hungry.*

You're always hungry. I pranced toward him, neck arched and front legs striking out playfully. *Come on, let's race! You know I'll win again!*

Tawil was a little lazy. But he could never resist a challenge. The other mares said it was because he was a colt, and that colts were like that. I wouldn't know—Tawil was the only male horse I knew in those early days.

You won't win this time, he warned me with a playful snort.

Giving a small buck, he took off across the oasis. I dug in and chased after him, sand flying from beneath my tiny, cuplike hooves.

The oasis where we lived was large and sprawling. A cool spring bubbled up from a depression in the dunes, forming a broad, shallow pool of fresh water. Craggy outcroppings nearby provided shade at certain times of the day, and we horses often napped there, though the camels preferred to rest beneath the tall, swaying palm trees that grew near the water. The large black woven tent where the humans lived stood on a hill with a view out into the desert, sheltered from the worst of the hot winds by the out-croppings. Birds and lizards flitted here and there, feeding on insects or the scrubby greenery of the oasis.

Despite my difficult start in life, I was growing up healthy and strong. That was a good thing, for the world in which we lived allowed for no weakness. Just outside the oasis lay the desert, vast dunes of sun-scorched sand that stretched to the horizon in every direction. As far as I knew then, that was all there was to the world. And it was enough for me. There was always something interesting to see or do.

Wake up, wake up! Tawil and I trumpeted as

we blasted into the area at the base of the rocks where the small herd of sheep and goats had bedded down the previous night.

The sheep reacted as they always did—they sprang to their feet and scattered before us, bleating with terror. Even at my tender age, I already knew that sheep were silly creatures who panicked at everything. The goats were a different story. Sometimes they ran with the sheep, while at other times they would stand their ground and try to butt us with their horns. But I didn't mind. That was all part of the fun. Besides, as agile and quick as the wily goats were, I was quicker still. It had been many days since any of the goats had been able to catch me.

As the sheep raced around like fools, the dogs started barking and rushed over to join us.

They were salukis, graceful creatures the color of the sand with long limbs and silky hair fringing their legs, tails, and ears. Even though the dogs were much smaller than horses, Jumanah had warned me and Tawil to respect them, for they were hunting animals with teeth that could hurt a horse.

But these dogs knew us and were our friends. Several half-grown puppies bounded out into the midst of the sheep stampede, pretending to nip at our heels, while Tawil and I pretended to kick out at them. We dashed up the hill, past the camels. There were five of them, large and calm with wise eyes and a strong smell. They didn't move as we frolicked past, merely chewing their cud and watching impassively while we raced around them.

One of the human women emerged from the tent just in time to see us run by, still pursued by the puppies. "Safiya!" she shouted through the veil that covered part of her face. "Hurry and come out. The foals are causing a commotion."

"Coming!"

Safiya popped out of the tent behind the woman. When I saw her, I skidded to a stop so fast that one of the pups bumped into my hind legs with a yelp of surprise.

But I ignored him. Safiya was my favorite of all the humans. She helped her mother and the other women care for us horses, though that was not the reason she was my favorite. My first clear memory had been of her kindness, and that made her special to me in a way I cannot explain.

"Settle down, Yatimah," the girl said with a

smile, reaching up to scratch me on my favorite spot between my ears. "Now come, we have something special to eat today."

Safiya, her mother, and the other women of the tribe were the ones who took care of the day-to-day needs of the animals. They milked the camels, gathered their dung for fuel, and made sure that all the creatures were healthy and content.

Today the women brought out a couple of baskets with some small brown fruits in them. I pricked my ears, flaring my large nostrils at the smell of the fruits. What were they?

Safiya laughed at my expression. "I think you're the most curious foal I've ever seen," she teased. "I expect you're wondering what we have here, aren't you? They're dates, just like the ones that grow on the trees. The grazing here is getting sparse for you horses, even though there's still plenty of scrub for the goats and camels. So we'll have to start giving you dates to fill you up until it's time to move on to rejoin our cousins at the next grazing spot."

Her mother shot her a bemused look. "Enough talking to the animals, daughter," she scolded. "There is work to do."

I watched as Safiya helped pour the dates onto the hard-packed sand. Jumanah and the other mares surged forward, nickering eagerly as they reached for the dates. Tawil and I stepped closer, both of us curious.

Come, little ones, Jumanah called to us. *These are good to eat.*

One of the other mares, a slender liver

chestnut known as Gameela, kicked out at a hungry goat that was sidling closer. *Yes, they're delicious*, the mare told Tawil and me. *Sweeter than the sweetest grass.*

That was all I needed to hear. Pushing my way between Jumanah and an older mare called Ajouz, I grabbed one of the dates. Its flavor burst in my mouth, moist and delicious. Dates were good!

I sampled one more, chewing it with gusto. Then a bird flew past, distracting me from the food. Prancing off after it, I ended up splashing in the cool water of the oasis just for the fun of seeing the water fly up around my feet. Tawil soon followed and joined in the game.

Jumanah and the other mares were still eating when Nasr appeared at the entrance to the tent.

He had his favorite falcon on his arm. He fussed with the bird's feathers, merely chuckling when the falcon snapped at him with its sharp, curved beak.

It looks as if Nasr is going hunting, Tawil observed. *Mama says he uses that falcon to catch other birds that the humans can eat. I wonder if he'll ride Zahrat again this time.*

I glanced at a horse standing with the others. She was tall for a mare, her coat the darkest bay with white coming halfway up all four legs and splashed onto her face. Her ears always seemed to be moving, swiveling about as if trying to hear everything that was happening in the entire desert, and her large eyes had a nervous expression.

Jumanah says Nasr wants to make Zahrat his

new war mare since she had no foal this year, I told Tawil. *But Zahrat doesn't think Nasr likes her.*

Mama says it's because Zahrat sees danger where there is none, Tawil reported. *That makes Nasr impatient with her, which only frightens her all the more.*

I wasn't sure what to think of that. But later, I watched as Nasr rode Zahrat off into the desert with his falcon on his arm. Safiya was watching, too. She came over and stood with one hand resting on my withers. Horse and man were only a few yards away when the falcon let out a sudden cry, making Zahrat jump to one side and start trembling.

"Oh, dear," Safiya murmured. "That will not make Father think any more highly of poor Zahrat. But she cannot help it if she is more

sensitive than the other mares." She bit her lip and looked down at me. "All he can think about is that she is nothing like Sarab. Then again, no horse in the camp is, at least in his eyes. . . ."

I didn't know what she meant. But her expression made me feel sad, so I let out a snort and reared up on my hind legs to make myself feel better. Within seconds, Safiya was laughing, and all was well again in my world.

A Desert Evening

One evening, a stronger breeze than usual blew through the oasis, making the air feel cool and pleasant even before the sun had begun to set. It tickled my ears and made me shake my head. That movement made it seem like a good idea to leap straight up in the air and kick out.

Oh, Yatimah, Jumanah said with a sigh. *Can you ever be still?*

You know she cannot, wise old Ajouz replied. *She is Sarab's foal, after all, and Sarab was just like her at that age. If Yatimah can learn to channel her energy as her mother did . . .*

Tawil blinked sleepily. He had already collapsed on the sand near his dam's feet. *Be quiet, Yatimah,* he complained. *I'm tired. Stop jumping around like a silly sheep.*

How dare you call me a sheep? I challenged him. I struck out at him with one foreleg, spraying sand in his face. That made him sneeze, and he let out an annoyed snort.

Safiya was just finishing with her chores. She laughed when she saw me dancing around the sleepy colt. "What's the matter, Yatimah?"

she asked. "Not ready for nighttime quite yet?"

She reached down and patted a ewe that was following her around. It head-butted her insistently, looking for more food.

"You'll have to find the rest of your dinner yourself, my woolly friend," the girl told the sheep with a fond smile. "Praise Allah, there is some grazing left for you yet, though the horses will be getting by on nothing but dates before long."

She gave the animal a slap on the rump, shooing it off after its herdmates, who were wandering toward their usual sleeping spot. Then she stood for a moment, watching a couple of goats snuffle among the stone for bits of grass and weeds. One of the salukis sat watching them as well, his ears and nose twitching with each shift of the wind.

I left Tawil alone and bounded over to Safiya. She gave me a pat. Another breeze gusted past, but this time I stayed still. The girl tipped her face up.

"That cool air feels good after this hot day." She glanced at the western sky. "There's still time for a walk. I think I spotted a patch of green just a little way out beyond the edge of the oasis. There must be another small spring there. Shall we see if there might be some extra grazing for you, little one?"

I pricked up my ears. Though I was getting better all the time at reading the humans' emotions and intentions, I still didn't understand most of what they said in their language. However, I was beginning to pick up the meaning of certain words. One of those words was *grazing*, which I understood to mean food. Not the rich, delicious milk that Jumanah was still providing for both Tawil and me, but the food that the adult horses ate—grasses and certain tasty weeds. The older I got, the more I appreciated grazing.

I followed willingly as Safiya wandered out into the desert, shading her eyes against the setting sun as she looked for the spot she wanted. Behind us drifted the sounds of human voices, the soft bleating of sheep and goats jostling for the best sleeping spots, and the occasional nicker of a horse, yip of a dog, or sigh of a camel. In other words, the ordinary evening sounds of the oasis.

But I paid little attention, staying focused on Safiya. She began a game we played often, stopping and starting and turning while encouraging me to follow her every step. I was good at the game. Watching her, anticipating her next movement, gave my lively mind something to focus on. Safiya hardly had to move a muscle before I was with her, my muzzle at her shoulder.

She finally tested me by turning in a complete circle. When I stayed right with her, pivoting my hind end around her, she laughed with delight. Then she looked around. We were perhaps a hundred paces out into the desert by now. The setting sun's rays washed the sand with gold and crimson.

"There it is." Safiya peered down the slope of the next dune. Here the sand had a green tinge. "There's not as much grass as I'd hoped. Still, it's something."

I saw the grass, too, and bounded forward to eat it. It was sparse, but it tasted delicious after several days of nothing but milk and dates and the occasional weed.

As I grazed, Safiya stroked me and worked a few twigs and burs out of my short mane. Then she ran her hands over my body, rubbing off bits of my foal coat to reveal the glossy black hair beneath. It felt so good that I stood there even after I'd eaten every blade of grass, simply enjoying the girl's company.

"I don't know why Father can't see how special you are," Safiya whispered after a few moments of silence. "I miss Sarab, too. But at least I have you to comfort me for missing her. Father won't even let himself have that. It's not fair to him, or to you."

She sighed loudly. I swiveled my head around so I could see her face, wondering what was wrong.

"Oh, Yatimah," she said, wrapping her arms around my neck. "Everyone says I mustn't pester Father about you. But how can he be so stubborn?"

A gust of wind chased the last of her words away and blew up under my tail, making me jump. Safiya blinked and looked around. Night falls quickly in the desert, and the sky was already washed with deepest indigo.

"We should get back," the girl said, glancing across the dunes toward the oasis. Someone had lit a lantern near the tent, and its light flickered and danced in the increasing breeze. The strains of lively music came from that way.

I lifted my head as my keen vision caught something strange in the opposite direction. It was farther out in the desert, a twisting, moving shape, larger than the largest camel. What could it be? I had no idea, but seeing it made me quiver with fear of the unknown.

"What is it, girl?" Safiya followed my gaze, then let out a gasp. "Oh no! A sandstorm!" she cried. "Hurry, we have to get back to camp!"

She turned and raced across the sand as fast as her human legs would take her. That wasn't very fast, but I forced myself to remain at a trot, not wanting to leave her behind.

Horses' eyes are set on the sides of our heads, which means we can see a good distance behind us. I could see that the sandstorm was gathering size and strength as it roared toward us. My body trembled, aching to burst into a gallop to try to escape the fearsome creature bearing down on us. But hearing Safiya's frightened panting as she ran, I knew I couldn't abandon her.

We struggled on together as the sandstorm reached us like some enormous, screaming falcon. Dust and sand swirled around us, getting into my eyes and nose and making it difficult to see or breathe. The air felt alive; it sent sparks crackling through me like during a lightning storm.

"I can't see!" Safiya cried, holding on to my mane for all she was worth. "Yatimah, I don't know which way to go! We'll be lost in the desert!"

The panic in her voice gripped my mind, causing me to tremble with fear. All I could think about was getting away from the terrible storm that was attacking us. For a moment, I nearly pulled free and galloped back to the camp, back to the safety of my familiar herd. There I could hide behind Jumanah's comforting bulk until the storm passed.

Instead, though, I forced myself to stay where I was. No matter what happened, I couldn't leave Safiya. Especially when I knew she was frightened.

This thought made me feel calmer. Whatever happened, we would be together to face it.

And so I kept my pace slow and steady. The swirling sand forced itself into my nostrils, trying to trap the breath within my body. But I put my head down to block the worst of the wind, and in that way I was able to breathe well enough to keep going. Beside me, I heard Safiya coughing with almost every step.

Home. I knew we needed to find our way home. We would be safe there in the shelter of the bluffs.

It was impossible to see anything more than a step ahead. The air was thick with grit and dust

and sand, like a living, churning wall blocking us
off from the entire world.

But I didn't need to see. My instincts told
me which way to go. I struggled on against the
wind, hardly feeling Safiya's hands clutching me,
though I knew she was there. Soon we were
almost at the edge of the trees.

I heard one of the other horses cry out in alarm. That made me cry out in return and leap forward in a sudden panic. In my eagerness I paid no attention to where I was going, and I felt my leg scrape across a stray boulder that I hadn't remembered was in our path. I staggered and almost fell, the howling sand stinging my eyes as they went wide with pain.

"Yatimah!" Safiya cried, her voice almost instantly whipped away by the wind. "Are you all right?"

My leg screamed with the impact, and for a moment I was ready to race off in any direction to try to escape the feeling. But Safiya was already bending over me, and so I forced myself to keep still, only turning my head away from the worst of the swirling wind. Sand pelted against me, adding to the pain in my leg, and I understood that I had to fight the urge to run. I had to trust Safiya. She would know what to do.

"You're bleeding," Safiya said in a voice tight with anxiety. She coughed again as another gust blew sand into her face and mine. "Come, we have to get you into the tent!"

4

Inside the Tent

"Safiya!" one of the men called out with relief as the girl and I burst into the tent, bringing a whoosh of wind and a cloud of dust from the sandstorm along with us. "When the storm blew in with the speed of a gazelle, we feared you were lost in it!"

"I'm all right." The young girl was panting with the exertion of fighting the wind. "But Yatimah is hurt. She spooked just as we got back and cut her leg on a rock."

I had never been inside the humans' tent before, though Jumanah had told me about it. It was a big, shadowy place lined with rugs and cushions and smelling strongly of the dark heated liquid the humans often drank. A falcon was perched upon a stick with a hood over its head; it turned its face toward us even though there was no way it could see us. Several dogs lounged near a small fire nearby. Nasr was sitting there as well, along with the other men of our camp. He looked up sharply at hearing my name, then frowned and turned away. But he said nothing as Safiya hurried me

past and through a flap into another section of the tent.

"Don't pay any attention to Father," she whispered to me. "I know he shows little care for you now. But it is only because he misses your mother so much. He'll come around after a while. . . ."

I hardly heard her. It was very strange being trapped within the woven walls, with more fabric blocking out all view of the sky overhead. Even the sounds of the storm were muffled in here. For a moment, I felt the urge to run, to fight my way back out into the openness of the oasis.

But then I felt Safiya's gentle hands upon me, and my mind cleared. I was with friends here. The humans had always taken care of me; they would allow no harm to come to me now.

I found myself in another large room. This

one was occupied by women and the younger children. The scents of human food hung in the air along with smoke from the fire. Soon I was surrounded by caring faces.

"What have we here?" one of the women asked. "Ah, Yatimah, I see your liveliness has gotten you into some trouble. Never mind, it's nothing serious. We'll just clean the wound and you'll be good as new in a week or so. . . ."

There was more, but the words mattered little to me. My eyes and ears drooped with relaxation as the human voices washed over me, soothing and familiar. I hardly even felt the sting as Safiya gently scrubbed out my wound and applied some sort of salve to it. Before long the pain and throbbing had faded enough for me to collapse onto the ground and drift off to sleep.

* * *

The next morning, Safiya led me out of the tent through the men's room. Nasr looked up from his breakfast as we passed.

"That filly going to be all right?" he asked gruffly.

"Yes, Father." Safiya smiled at him hopefully. "Yatimah is a strong foal. Just like Sarab was. I know she's going to make just as fine a war mare one day."

"We'll see." The man ran his eyes over me. "Sarab once carried me through a terrible sand-storm for nearly an hour without ever hesitating or taking a wrong step. Or spooking at a rock, of all things."

I was feeling impatient to get back outside. Wriggling beneath Safiya's hands, I lunged toward the tent opening, my nostrils seeking the fresh air and my stomach crying out for Jumanah's milk.

"Wait, little one," Safiya told me, trying to hang on to my short mane.

"Skittish, is she?" Nasr's frown deepened. "Not like her dam in that way, either."

"She's not skittish," Safiya said. "Just full of energy, that's all."

Nasr stood and followed us out of the tent. I let out a whinny as I spotted the other horses drinking at the edge of the spring. Tawil heard me, his head shooting up as he returned my call.

"Too bad the only other foal we got this year was that colt," Nasr said. "Still, I suppose I can make do with Zahrat for a while. Or perhaps I can get Jumanah back into shape once the foals are weaned. . . ."

I heard no more as I raced off to join the herd. Later, though, I remembered the sad look on Safiya's face at her father's words.

Why does Nasr always frown when he looks at me? I asked that evening after Tawil and I had eaten some dates and then drunk our fill of Jumanah's milk.

Jumanah blew a long sigh out of her large nostrils. *The ways of humans are a mystery,* she said. *But I do know that Sarab was very special to Nasr. She was his favorite war mare.*

Are you a war mare, Mama? Tawil asked.

I was the war mare of Nasr's son Basim before I became too heavy with foal, Jumanah replied.

Now Basim rides Gameela, so I suppose I am just a mare again.

But what does a war mare do that just a mare doesn't? I asked.

The men ride the war mares when they raid other men's camps, Jumanah said.

Raid? Tawil echoed. *What does that mean?*

The sound of Nasr's voice interrupted our discussion. He appeared with two of his sons at his side, all of them talking in loud, excited voices.

What's going on? I asked.

Hush, little ones, Jumanah responded. *Just stay out of their way and you shall see all in time.*

I watched as Nasr saddled and mounted Zahrat, while his sons prepared their own mares,

Gameela and Ibtisam. Tawil looked as perplexed
as I.

Where are they going? he asked as horses and
riders disappeared into the darkening desert.

Do not worry, Jumanah told us. *They will return soon enough. Then you will understand what I mean by a raid.*

She refused to say any more. Several hours passed, enough for me to forget about the mystery of the humans' behavior and drift off to sleep, even though it felt strange to have part of our herd missing.

I was startled awake by shouts and the thunder of hooves. Scrambling to my feet, I saw men and horses galloping into the oasis. Basim and his brother were laughing and shouting, though Nasr was quiet. All three mares looked weary, but they started prancing with excitement when they saw us watching. There was a bleating lamb slung across the front

of Zahrat's saddle, while Ibtisam was carrying
two young goats.

Then my eyes widened as I saw that these
were not the only strange new creatures with
them. Gameela's rider was leading an unfamiliar
mare beside her!

5

New Experiences

I do not understand, I told Jumanah, who was watching along with Tawil, Ajouz, and me. *Where did that horse come from?*

The newcomer was a shiny bay with a tiny star peeking out from beneath her long, silky forelock. Her legs were slender but strong, her body compact and graceful, her tail full and glossy.

Old Ajouz heard my question and responded with excitement in her eyes. *We took her in a raid. She will be part of our herd now.*

As far as I knew until that moment, my herdmates and I were the only horses in existence. Seeing this bay mare was a strange new experience for me. However, the strangeness soon gave way to curiosity. The humans seemed to be curious, too. Safiya, her mother, and the other women emerged from the tent along with the men who hadn't gone on that night's raid. They all exclaimed over the new animals.

The bay mare stared around with wide, anxious eyes as the men released her and the other mares. When Jumanah took a step toward

her, the newcomer flared her nostrils. Jumanah lowered her head and snaked it forward, flattening her ears. The new mare lowered her own head in submission, taking a step backward.

Then Ajouz came forward, prancing in a way I had never seen the old mare do before. Zahrat, Tawil, and I crowded along at her hip, heads up and eyes excited.

Meanwhile the humans were chasing the new lamb and goats off to join their own herds. Then they stood and watched us horses for a few minutes before heading for the tent.

"Will they be all right, Father?" Safiya asked with a yawn.

"Don't worry, child. They'll sort things out on their own." Nasr patted her on the shoulder.

I hardly noticed when the humans disappeared into their tent. I was busy watching the new mare. She was submissive to the rest of the herd. She only wanted to fit in and had no wish to fight. For a while Zahrat and Gameela seemed interested in chasing the newcomer around just for fun, but wise old Ajouz soon put a stop to that.

By dawn, we were all dozing together near the water's edge. The bay mare was already becoming friendly with Ibtisam, who chased off Zahrat and Gameela anytime they got too close.

Safiya emerged from the tent bright and early. She brought us all dates, making sure the newcomer got her share.

"Aren't you pretty?" she crooned as she patted the bay mare. "Father says you are to be called Hasna. I think it suits you."

I snorted, impatient for the girl's attention. Frolicking closer, I kicked out at Hasna. She backed away at once, though I had to dodge an annoyed bite from Ibtisam. But Safiya chased off both mares with a wave of her hand.

"Good morning, Yatimah." The girl greeted me with her usual pats and scratches. "I hope you'll be nice to the new horse. It is an honor for Father to have taken such a fine animal, with Allah's blessing."

I didn't know what she meant, or much care, either. All I wanted was her attention, which I enjoyed until Safiya's mother called her off to help with the camels.

Later that day, the heat of the midday desert sun chased us into the shade as usual. At first Zahrat and Gameela seemed ready to keep Hasna away from the outcroppings. But Ibtisam squealed her protest, crowding them back so her new friend could creep into the shade.

Enough, you two, Ajouz scolded when she saw what was going on. *Hasna is one of us now.*

Jumanah agreed in her calm way. *Yes. And she is not trying to take anyone's place in the herd, so there's no purpose in fighting.*

That's right, Hasna said in her submissive way. *I do not wish to cause any trouble.*

But I still don't understand, I burst out. *How did you come here?*

Hasna looked at me. *I lived in another herd until last night. A larger one—twice as many mares as here, plus some foals and two stallions. Then you arrived carrying your humans. . . .* She bowed her head toward Zahrat, Gameela, and Ibtisam.

They grabbed me and led me off with their ropes. I thought my friend Bayda was coming, too. But she pulled away when the dogs barked and ran back to camp.

Yes. Ibtisam shot a look in Zahrat's direction. *Someone nickered, which alerted the dogs at that camp, along with their humans.*

I was frightened, Zahrat responded. *It was dark, and I smelled the other horses, and I couldn't resist calling to them. . . .*

Never mind, Jumanah put in. Seeing that Tawil and I were still confused, she did her best to explain. *Now and then the humans decide to ride fast across the desert and raid each other's camps, taking as many animals as they can. I have been on many such raids myself.*

As have I, Gameela said. *And I was born*

with different humans, just like Hasna. Nasr raided my home camp when I was only a yearling.

Tawil looked more and more alarmed by the whole story. *But why do they do it?* he wondered. *All this galloping across the desert sounds so tiring. Why don't all the animals just stay where they are born?*

As I have told you before, the ways of humans are a mystery, Jumanah told him. *But as long as they take care of us, it is of no importance to us horses.*

I looked out into the desert, feeling strangely excited by all this talk of raids. Was this what my mother had done? What would it be like to race swiftly and silently across the sand under cover of darkness, as she must have? To return with more horses and other animals for the camp? It was a strange idea, but a thrilling one.

Despite the heat of the sun, I couldn't resist stepping out of the shade for a better look across the dunes. As I wandered around, my mind full of Hasna's tale, I found myself near the tent. Nasr and his eldest son, Basim, were outside watching the goats drink from the spring.

"It is too bad that Allah frowned upon our raid this time," Basim was saying. "I cannot recall the last time we returned with less. Only one lamb, a couple of goats, and the mare. And no camels at all, even though Dirar's people have at least a dozen!"

"It was not Allah who doomed us last night." Nasr's voice was hard. "It was that nervous, skittish fool of a mare. Zahrat was nearly as noisy as a stallion when we approached the other camp!"

His son sighed. "I suppose you're right.

Perhaps we'll have to put Jumanah back to work earlier than planned. The foals should be weaned soon in any case."

"Perhaps. Or perhaps this new bay mare will do." Suddenly Nasr turned and saw me wandering nearby. He frowned, his eyes going dark. "If only we had not lost Sarab . . ."

I took a step toward him, ears pricked forward as I recognized my dam's name. But Nasr turned away and strode off, his robes swishing around him.

A few days later, I awoke to find a new air of excitement about the camp. The humans were all up early and bustling around with raised voices and active eyes. The sheep were jittery and kept bumping into each other, causing more than one of them to be head-butted by an impatient goat. The dogs had caught the mood, too, and barked at the smallest things.

What is it? I asked, already feeling keyed up.

Tawil, as usual, was slow to awaken. *Is something happening?* he wondered lazily as he blinked and looked around. *Was there another raid?*

Jumanah didn't respond for a moment. She was watching the humans carefully. Then she looked over at Ajouz. *Is it what I think it is?* she asked the older mare.

I believe so, Ajouz responded.

What? I danced in place, unable to fight the agitation I felt in the air. *What is it? What's happening?*

Something new for you, little ones, Jumanah told Tawil and me. *It is time for us to move on!*

Moving On

At first I didn't understand what Jumanah meant. *Move on?*

But Jumanah did her best to explain it, with help from Ajouz and the other mares. They told us that every so often, the humans would pack up everything they had and move to a different oasis with more greenery for the animals and fruit for the humans. Sometimes they would join other parts of their human tribe in the new place, and we animals would mingle together in larger herds until it was time to move on again. And so I began to understand that the time had come to leave the place where I was born.

I was just as surprised by this as I had been by Hasna's arrival. There had been no reason to think that there were any other oases besides this one, or that we would ever have reason to leave here. But now that it was happening, I was eager to find out more. What would the new oasis be like? Would there be fresh grass for nibbling?

I am ready to leave right now! I told Tawil, frolicking around him in a circle.

He stood and watched me, his ears flopping

lazily to either side. *I hope it is not a long walk*, he said. *But more food would be nice, I suppose.*

The humans rushed to pack up their encampment before the full heat of the sun arrived. They saddled all of the horses except Tawil and me, along with one of the camels. The remaining camels' backs were loaded with the dismantled tent and the rest of the humans' possessions.

Finally it was time to go. The men swung aboard their usual mounts, while Safiya's grandmother rode Ajouz, one of her aunts rode Jumanah, and a few of the smaller children climbed onto the camel with one of their uncles. Safiya and the rest of the older children went on foot, along with the remaining adults.

With help from the dogs, the humans herded the goats and sheep together, and we set out into the desert.

It was all very exciting to me, as new experiences always were. I was near the middle of the caravan, trotting circles around Jumanah. It wasn't until I saw the gray mare glance back at our oasis that I thought to do the same myself. It already looked strange and empty without the big black tent and the circle of camels lounging beneath the nodding palms. It was odd to think of leaving it, but exciting to wonder what lay ahead.

Soon the oasis was out of sight behind us. Being out in the open, empty desert was new and exhilarating. I couldn't help kicking up

my heels now and then from the sheer thrill of
it all.

Settle down, little one, Jumanah told me after
a while. *You don't want to wear yourself out.*

I'm not tired, I retorted. *Come on, Tawil—
let's race to the front of the line!*

We took off bucking and playing, dashing

past Nasr, who was riding Zahrat at the head of the line. He yelled at us, but we hardly noticed. This was an exciting new adventure, and we could hardly contain ourselves!

The caravan trudged on through the desert, the rest of the animals pacing themselves by the camels' measured gait. All I could see in every direction was sand rolling off toward the horizon in softly undulating dunes. The sun climbed higher in the clear pale sky, beating down upon us, with neither trees to shade us nor cool springwater to refresh us.

Once our early burst of energy passed, Tawil and I slowed to a walk. He plodded along on one side of Jumanah and I on the other, my dragging feet kicking up little puffs of sand with each step.

When will we reach the new oasis? Tawil complained. *I am thirsty!*

And I am hungry, I added.

Be patient, little ones, Jumanah told us. *We shall arrive when we arrive. Until then, we walk on as long as the humans tell us to do so.*

I noted that her neck and flanks were slick with sweat. The sheep and goats dragged along with lowered heads, the humans looked weary, and even the dogs' tails drooped lower than they had at the beginning of the journey. Only the camels seemed untroubled by the harsh environment and the long walk. They ambled along with their strange, shuffling gait, their fringed eyes always on the horizon.

After a while, we stopped. I looked around hopefully, but there was no water in sight, nor any trees or other signs of an oasis.

"I think I will walk for a bit," said Safiya's aunt, who had been riding Jumanah. "This mare is thin from nursing two foals; I'm sure she could use a rest."

"Indeed." Nasr glanced toward Tawil and me with a slight frown. "We shall all walk."

Everyone except the small children on the

camel dismounted. Then we continued on our way, with most of the humans walking along beside the animals.

I wish we would reach the new oasis soon, Tawil grumbled to me after another hour.

Yes, I agreed.

But Jumanah didn't join in our complaints, and neither did the other horses. Even the silly sheep seemed content to toil along willingly, stride after stride. And of course the camels never wavered.

If they could do it, I knew that I could as well. I lifted my feet a little higher, step-step-step-step, each hoof picking itself up as another touched down, walking with long strides to match those of the adult horses. Before long I settled into a rhythm, and my muscles began to hum with the exercise. I was still tired, but being tired no longer felt like a bad thing. In fact, it was satisfying to look ahead and see all that sand, the desert just waiting for me to stride along and conquer it with my steady gait. . . .

For once my mind wasn't racing faster than I could follow. All my focus was on putting one foot in front of the other, of completing this journey no matter how long and tiring it might turn out to be. Even the heat ceased to be a nuisance; the sweat coating my body felt good.

We finally stopped when the sun was almost touching the western horizon. There was still no sign of an oasis. But the humans had packed dates for us to eat and camel's milk for us to drink. Tawil and I were able to slake our thirst with some of Jumanah's milk as well, though she was producing less with each passing day. I was still hungry and thirsty when I finished. But there was nothing to be done about that, as Jumanah was quick to tell me when I complained.

A moment later, Safiya found me. "Don't worry, Yatimah. The next oasis is my favorite of all. When we arrive there, we'll all have plenty to eat and drink, and we'll be reunited with our cousins, and there will be much celebrating," she whispered. Then she opened her tightly clenched hand, revealing a few dates. "Here—I saved these from my lunch. They're for you."

I eagerly gobbled down the extra dates and snuffled at the girl's hands and face, hoping for more. She giggled and gave me a hug. Then her

father called to her, and she had to hurry away
to help the other humans.

Soon the camels and the adult horses were
hobbled, and the dogs had gathered the sheep
and goats into a tight herd near the humans'
campfire. I collapsed wearily onto the warm

sand near the rest of the herd. It had been a long, exhausting day, and I was asleep almost instantly.

I was startled awake sometime after dark by the sudden, urgent barking of the dogs. By the time I scrambled to my feet, my heart pounding with fear, the men were shouting. Zahrat let out a whinny of terror. There was a thunder of hooves and the cry of unfamiliar human voices.

For a second, I had no idea what was happening. I could only stand there stock-still, every muscle in my body quivering. In the darkness, I saw the other horses rushing around in a panic despite their hobbles.

Then Nasr's voice rang out, harsh with anger. "To arms!" he shouted. "We are being raided!"

Memories and Changes

I spun around, whinnying anxiously for Jumanah and the rest of the herd. There was a flash of silvery mane, and I saw a moon-gray mare I didn't recognize. A human clung to her back; as I watched, he leaned over and grabbed a lamb off the ground. For a moment, he stared directly at me, his face calculating. But then he turned away and let out a shout.

"Away!" he cried out. "They're awake!"

The silvery mare whirled and raced off as swiftly as the desert wind itself, the lamb bleating piteously from her back. I blinked into the darkness, able to spy only vague shapes disappearing into the night.

That was when Jumanah found me. *Are you all right, little one?* she wanted to know as she nosed me from head to toe.

What has happened? I asked her, my heart still beating fast from the commotion.

It was a raid, she told me. *Just as our humans raided another camp to bring us Hasna, so have these other humans raided us in turn. They probably saw that we were travelers and not ready to defend ourselves.*

I soon discovered that she was right. The raiders had spotted us from a distance as we'd passed through their territory earlier that day. They had come to us under the cover of darkness and escaped with one of our camels, half a dozen sheep . . . and Tawil.

When I noticed that the colt was among the animals taken, I refused to accept it at first. I raced around the temporary camp, calling for him while searching among the goats and beneath the camels for his familiar chestnut form. But he was nowhere to be found, and soon I realized there was no point in such efforts. His absence saddened me, though most of the humans seemed far more upset about the loss of the camel.

"At least they didn't get any of the mares,"

one man said. "Allah be praised it was only the colt who was taken."

"Yes," Basim responded. "Poor Jumanah will be better off for having one fewer mouth to feed."

"Indeed." Nasr turned to stare at me thoughtfully by the light of the fire. "I suppose it's a blessing that it was the colt and not the filly."

Drawn by his gaze, I walked toward him and nosed at his robes. He dropped one hand briefly onto my withers before abruptly turning and hurrying away.

Two days later, we finally reached the new oasis. It was even larger and more pleasant than the one we'd left, with a waterfall tumbling down a rocky cliff and plenty of grass coating the banks of the large spring. Other humans were already there, and they let out cries of joy when they spotted us approaching. These were Nasr's cousins, who had gone their own way during the driest months. They hurried to help our humans set up their tent, while all the animals got acquainted with the other group's herds and then chose their favorite spots to eat and rest.

We horses found ourselves in the company of Cousin Rami's horses, which numbered four mares, along with a yearling filly and an adult stallion known as Majeeb. These horses recognized all except Hasna and me from the last time the families had camped together, so it didn't take long until we were all one large, happy herd. Once a month or two had passed, it was as if we'd never lived anywhere else.

The grazing helped me grow taller and

stronger. My foal fuzz was gone by now, replaced by a sleek coat of glossy black. Eventually Jumanah began turning away when I tried to nurse, and after a while, I didn't even miss her milk. The fresh grass and the cool springwater were all I needed, though Safiya often brought me dates and other little treats.

Sometimes Safiya would clench both fists and hold them out to me, wanting me to guess which one held my treat. It was easy for me to locate the date or other morsel by smell, though it seemed to delight the girl no end when I would nose at the correct hand. Sometimes, too, she would want me to perform some little task or movement before I got my treat. Once I picked up the foot she grasped, or bowed my head, or allowed her to drape a cloth on my back, she

would feed me the treat and then scratch and praise me with great enthusiasm. Her happy words at these times were of nearly the same value to me as the food itself, for I enjoyed pleasing her.

One day, when we were playing these games, I noticed Nasr watching us from over near the tents. His face wore a thoughtful expression.

I pricked my ears toward him. Safiya turned to see what I was looking at and spotted him as well.

"Look, Father!" she called. "See how fast Yatimah learns things? She is the smartest filly I've known!"

"Hmm" was all Nasr said in response. Then he turned to shoo one of the dogs away from the tents.

During this time, Nasr started to ride Jumanah. She always did her best to please him, and the more he rode her the stronger she became. One day, they returned from a ride while Safiya was picking knots out of my tail, which had become tangled during my last vigorous roll in the sand.

"How is Jumanah doing, Father?" she asked.

"As well as can be expected." Nasr patted the gray mare, then swung down from the saddle. "I only wish she were faster." He sighed, sounding dissatisfied.

"I'm sure she goes as fast as she can," Safiya said. "She is of heavier build than Sarab was, after all."

At that moment, one of the dogs barked, and I saw the sheep start to run around in circles, bleating with panic. I spun to face them, my muscles quivering as I wondered whether I should race over and join them. It was only the sheep being silly, so I stayed where I was, but Nasr looked at me with a frown.

"At least Jumanah has a good, steady temperament," he muttered, giving the mare another pat as she stood quietly by his side. "That is a blessing from Allah."

The next two or three years passed in much the same way. We horses have little concept of time, and I soon lost track of how often we moved to a new oasis. Sometimes we joined camps with other humans from Nasr's family, and at other times it was just us. Often the humans would trade among themselves or with passing travelers, which meant the herds of sheep and goats were always changing, and often some of the puppies would go off to a new home when they were old enough. During the second season that we camped with Rami's clan, we found that he had taken two new mares in a raid and had traded one of his camels for a young stallion that both he and Nasr would be able to use for breeding.

But our own little herd of horses remained the same, so I didn't worry much about any of that. Moving every so often began to feel as natural a part of life as eating and sleeping.

I had grown into a strong, graceful mare, sound of limb and wind. When I was old enough, Basim began my training. Thanks to the little games Safiya had taught me, it was easy for me to understand what he wanted most of the time.

Before long he was riding me around our current oasis home and out for short distances into the desert, and he seemed well pleased by my progress.

One day, as we returned from such a desert ride, my pace quickened. I had caught the scent of something new—a camel, but not one of ours. What was a strange camel doing in our oasis? I guessed right away that it had to be a traveler, perhaps part of a caravan passing through.

"What is it, Yatimah?" Basim asked, giving me a pat.

I could not answer him except by pricking my ears toward the strange scent. A moment later, he could see the unfamiliar camel for himself. It was lowering itself onto the sand near the tent, looking sandblown and weary. A man slid down from its back as we approached. I was

surprised to see that he and his camel were alone, for in the desert, most humans travel in groups for safety.

Then I caught the traveler's scent and saw his face, which looked as weary as his camel's. I let out a trumpet of alarm, for I had a good memory. Though I did not know the camel, I recognized this man.

It was the stranger who had ridden into our temporary camp in the desert some years back aboard a pale gray mare—one of the raiders who had taken Tawil and the other animals!

Visitors and Decisions

The man stepped over and touched one of the poles of the tent just as Basim brought me to a stop and dismounted.

"Greetings, stranger," he said.

"Greetings," the man replied in a voice coarse with desert grit and thirst. "I am lost, and my camel is exhausted. By the mercy and blessings of Allah, will you give me shelter and water?"

Basim shouted for Nasr, then nodded. "Of course you are welcome as our esteemed guest," he said. "Please come inside, and I'll have the women see to your camel."

Safiya came to untack me while Basim and the other men welcomed the visitor. "I am glad that man has come in peace this time," she murmured into my ear. "Every time there is a raid, I fear someone will take you. And I fear even more that Father would not try to get you back."

As soon as she released me, I trotted over to Jumanah. She was standing near the waterfall nursing her current foal, a lively colt who was already turning gray like his dam.

Why is that man here, and why do our humans not chase him off and add his camel to our herd? I asked Jumanah. Do they not realize he is the one who raided us?

Oh, I am sure they realize it, Jumanah replied.

But human herds are ruled by many strange customs. Nasr and his family are bound by honor to welcome anyone into their home who asks for their help. And likewise, that man would do the same if they came to his camp.

I suppose that is not so strange, I responded thoughtfully. *It is much like the way we accepted Hasna into our herd, even though she was a stranger to us when she first came. Or the way Majeeb and his herd always welcome us whenever we rejoin them. Still, it does seem strange after what happened with Tawil. . . .*

Who is Tawil? the foal asked, looking up, his tiny muzzle smeared with milk.

Another hungry colt, like you, Jumanah told him fondly. *Now hurry and drink your fill so I can go and graze.*

The foal looked confused as he glanced over at the fillies born that year to Hasna and Ibtisam. I could tell he had no idea what colt his dam meant. Just like me at that age, he knew nothing of the larger world beyond our oasis.

But I left it to Jumanah to explain it to him as I trotted off toward the grass, still filled with wonder and confusion at the ways of the humans.

More time passed, and my training with Basim continued. Soon I knew to walk, trot, canter, gallop, and halt at the merest hint of his aids. I could tell he was pleased with me by the way he chuckled and patted me throughout our rides, and it pleased me a great deal to please him.

After a while, he began teaching me something new. When we returned to camp after a ride into the desert, the other horses often nickered to me, and I would usually return their greeting. However, Basim made it known that he did not wish me to do so.

"You must learn to be quiet if you are to be a good war mare like your mother," he told me sternly as he spun me away and put me into a tight circle after one such nicker. "Otherwise the noise might alert the sleeping encampment we are trying to raid, and that would do us no good at all." Moving so quickly in such a small circle was difficult and uncomfortable for me, which made me understand that Basim was unhappy with what I'd just done.

After that, each time I nickered to the others he would let me know it was not what he wanted. It wasn't long before I understood that

I was never to speak to the other horses while he was riding me. From then on, I was as silent as I could be. And that pleased Basim as well.

There were other lessons to learn. He taught me to remain steady beneath him even when his brothers threw stones at me. The first few times it was impossible not to react, though I did not panic and was careful not to unseat him. Finally I learned to withstand the unpleasant stinging of the stones and continue in whichever direction and at whatever gait my rider requested of me. Knowing how pleased Basim was when I did this gave me so much satisfaction that after a while, I barely felt the sting of the stones anymore.

Once Basim rode me out of camp beside one of his brothers on Gameela. Each man carried a young goat in front of him and several camel skins and some woven goods draped behind. In this way we traveled a great distance. This pleased me, as I enjoyed nothing more than the feeling of the desert sand passing beneath my hooves.

Finally we came within view of something very strange. A number of dark shapes rose from the desert—like tents, but larger and made of some odd substance.

I let out a snort of surprise as soon as Basim dismounted—for I knew better than to make a sound while he was on my back. *What can this place be?* I asked Gameela.

I have seen this place before, she told me. *It is a place where humans live who do not travel as ours do, but rather live in the same oasis all the time. They call it a town.*

The town was very odd indeed. There were

countless humans wandering around everywhere, along with a great quantity of dogs, camels, and other creatures of every description. Basim took the goats and the other items and hurried off, while his brother led Gameela and me to a trough to drink. The water tasted mustier than that of the clear desert springs I was used to, but after a few snorts of surprise I decided the difference was not worth worrying about when I was thirsty.

After that I stayed busy looking around at all the new sights. Other horses pranced past with their riders, and one stallion stopped to call to us, though his rider scolded him and urged him on. A boy passed by, driving some odd birds before him in a flock. Several people stopped to ask Basim's brother about our breeding, which humans always seemed to enjoy discussing at great length, or to talk with him about other matters.

Finally Basim returned. He no longer had the goats and other items, but was carrying two large bags.

"We did well today, brother," Basim called out, sounding cheerful. "Yusri was pleased with the kids and was generous with his flour and spices in trade. And I exchanged the skins for some fresh vegetables and other things that will make the women happy."

"Good." His brother squinted up at the sun. "The horses should be rested enough. We'd better go if we wish to be home by nightfall."

We set out again across the desert, reaching our oasis just as the sun disappeared from view

over the distant horizon. Safiya was waiting for us, ready to help take care of me after the long ride.

During these days I continued to see much of her. She was growing up into a fine young lady, old enough now to wear a veil like her mother and older sisters, but she was always quick to volunteer to care for me after a ride or training session. She was better than anyone else at brushing every speck of desert dust out of my glossy coat and rubbing my legs until they no longer felt weary. Though I was quite fond of Basim, it was Safiya whose company I sought over all others.

One day, more strangers arrived at the encampment. There were several of them this time, all looking sun-scorched and exhausted.

They were traveling on foot, except for one old man who rode a scruffy camel.

"We are pilgrims making our way to Mecca, if Allah wills it," the old man croaked out. "We have not come across another oasis for many days and are nearly out of water."

"You are welcome here, my friends," Nasr told them with a polite bow. "Please come inside for some refreshment."

"May Allah bestow his blessings upon you!" the man exclaimed in relief, while his companions murmured their own gratitude.

Soon the camel was resting in the shade and the humans were inside the tent. They emerged after a while and made their way over to us, with Nasr and the old man at the front of the group.

"Indeed, your herd is even finer than you

described," the old man said as he looked us over. "The gray broodmare is as stout and sturdy as can be, and the two chestnuts quite elegant." He turned to gaze at me. "As for your young black mare with the look of a falcon—why, she is the finest horse I have had the pleasure to see in some time."

"Thank you. I am honored by your compliments, my friend." Nasr's gaze wandered over me as well, his eyes troubled.

"Come," Basim said, putting out a hand to guide the strangers along. "Let me show you our equally fine camels."

The group moved on toward the spot where the camels were resting near the water. But Nasr lingered behind the others, still studying me with that troubled gaze. Safiya emerged to dump some old tea water and spotted him standing there.

"What is it, Father?" she asked, stepping toward him.

He turned away, and for a moment it seemed he would choose not to answer her. But then he turned abruptly and nodded toward me.

"Basim says Sarab's daughter has been doing well in her training," he said. "I have decided to give her a chance. I'm going to see if I can make your Yatimah into my new war mare."

9

Getting Acquainted

Nasr came to find me as soon as the pilgrims left. He strode up to me as I grazed beside Hasna, taking me by the halter and leading me toward the tent. At first I was wary, prancing a bit rather than walking along obediently as I always did for Basim or Safiya.

As I have said, I have a good memory. While Nasr had never treated me unkindly, he had never shown me any fondness whatsoever. Quite the contrary. Every time I had tried to approach him, he had turned away and remained aloof. How could I not be surprised that he was showing me this attention all of a sudden? Perhaps a horse like calm Jumanah would not react to something like that, but I had never been as placid as she.

"Hold still," Nasr growled after a few steps, yanking at my halter. "Do not make me regret this decision. You look so much like Sarab that it will make it all the worse if—"

He cut himself off. I had thrown my head up at his yank, but now I lowered it again, glancing at him cautiously. Sometimes I seemed able to read the humans' thoughts and emotions almost as clearly as those of my own kind, even though humans offered little of the same clarity in their body language. However, Nasr was different from Safiya or Basim or the others. He had always closed himself off to me. Why should I trust him now?

But Basim and Safiya had trained me well. I stood mostly still while Nasr put on my saddle and bridle. And I only pranced a little as he swung aboard. As he settled into the saddle, I went still again, waiting for his direction. He pressed his legs against my sides, and I walked forward. But my neck was up and tense, since I still felt wary.

At first he returned my wariness in kind. His aids were abrupt and felt unfamiliar. When he patted or praised me, it did not feel natural as it did coming from Safiya, Basim, or any of the others. It was as if he was forcing himself to be kind to me.

However, he kept trying. Throughout that ride and the next several, he stayed calm and patient, testing my reactions and my gaits.

With each ride, I relaxed more and more. Though I couldn't yet feel true affection from him, I could sense that he was trying as well as he knew how to form a bond with me. And if he was willing to try, I would try also. In fact, I was eager to do so. What need had I to know the reason for his change of heart? I would accept it, no matter where it had come from, much the way the humans themselves accepted travelers into their home with no questions asked.

And so the two of us had begun our training together. It wasn't always easy. Nasr's hand was heavier than his son's and his corrections less gentle. Whenever we galloped, he would pull me to a stop with the reins, even though all Basim had needed was a shift in weight. As much as I tossed my head to show my discomfort, he continued to do it.

"Stop fussing, will you?" he exclaimed at one such time. Through the reins, I felt his grip tighten and I quickly lifted my nose higher, anticipating a harder pull on my mouth.

But it didn't come. Nasr's hands relaxed again, and he sighed. "You're not Sarab," he muttered under his breath. "Allah forgive me, I should not expect you to be her. You can only be yourself, after all, like any of us."

He leaned forward and stroked my neck beneath my silky black mane. I relaxed, lowering my head and blowing out through my nostrils. I was beginning to see that while Nasr's punishments were swifter than Basim's, they were always fair. He didn't allow himself to react in anger, but only to guide me to do better.

And before long his praise came more often than the punishments. I started to anticipate what he would ask of me before he had to ask it, just as I had with Basim. Nasr barely had to close his legs to send me into a brisk trot or rolling canter. He no longer needed to pull on the reins to slow me or bring me to a halt. I would react to the merest shift in weight, offering what he wanted before his own muscles had fully formed the aid. We were functioning as one—one body, one mind.

After an especially good ride, he slid down and came to my head. "I can see I was wrong about you, my beautiful one," he said quietly. "The blood of a thousand generations of great war mares runs in your veins. How could I ever think you would not be worthy of Sarab's lineage? After all, she sacrificed her life to bring you into this world. . . ."

Lifting his hand, he rubbed my broad forehead. I lowered my face toward him, allowing my eyes to fall half-closed and my lower lip to droop. I leaned into him as he ran his hands up over my poll and down my crest, scratching all the itchy spots. In that moment, there was neither

past nor future, herdmates nor oasis. I was content just being there with my human.

After that, I began to seek Nasr out almost as eagerly as I did Safiya. I nickered if he walked past the herd, and if he stopped and looked at me, I went to him. He rewarded me with pats and kind words. True, he was never as expressive as Safiya or even Basim. But I could read what was in his heart, and that was far more important.

Time passed. One evening, as the moon climbed the night sky, I saw a flare of firelight as the tent flap opened. A moment later, Nasr and his three older sons made their way into the herd on feet as quick and silent as a saluki's. Basim went to Zahrat and began preparing her to ride, while his brothers did the same with Hasna and Ibtisam.

Meanwhile Nasr came to me. "Now we shall see what you are made of, my beauty," he whispered as he brushed the sand from my back. "We need more sheep. It is time to go get some."

The Raid

Soon the four of us horses were cantering across the desert with the men on our backs. The moon was nothing but a sliver, but horses see quite well in the dark and so our hoofbeats were steady and sure.

Is this a raid? I asked the others in the silent language of horses.

Indeed, it must be, Ibtisam replied. *That is the only reason the humans ride us out so far into the desert after nightfall.*

A little thrill ran through me, and I was tempted to throw my head downward and my heels upward in a buck of excitement. But I understood from my training that the humans did not like us to buck while they were riding us, and so I settled for an extra burst of speed.

Nasr laughed as he slowed me down again. "My new war mare seems eager for this adventure," he called to his sons. "It will be interesting to see if she does well tonight."

"She is Sarab's daughter," Basim replied.

"Of course she will do well. How could she not?"

"Hmm," Nasr responded, then fell silent.

I hope it is not a raid, Zahrat told us with a toss of her head. Her nostrils were flared more than they should have been for the easy exercise, and her eyes rolled so much that the whites glinted in the weak moonlight. *I do not like raids.*

Indeed, Zahrat had not been on a raid in a long time. It was only because Jumanah had a brand-new filly at her side and Gameela was due to foal any day that Basim had started riding the high-strung dark bay again. I felt sorry for Zahrat, knowing she was a nervous horse who seemed ill suited to this sort of work. But I found it impossible to focus on that, my mind being filled with the coming adventure. What would it be like?

We rode for several hours. My muscles hummed as the desert flew by beneath my hooves, and that helped my mind to settle. For a while I even forgot why we were out and merely enjoyed the exercise.

Then I caught the faint scent of smoke on the breeze. *I smell a human camp*, I said. *We must be close.*

The men must have known it, too. They soon slowed us to a trot and then a walk. They also stopped talking to each other, communicating only with soft whistles.

Excitement surged through me. Though this was my first raid as a war mare, being there felt familiar and good. Was it the blood of my dam, Sarab, guiding me, as the men thought? I recalled that early memory of her fine, chiseled head on the sand, the stories Nasr still told of their adventures together, and thought that it must be so.

In any event, I knew that this was where I was meant to be, the reason I had been born, generations of war mares coursing through my blood. I was the product of their lives and experiences as well as the training I had received from my humans and from the desert itself.

It felt right. And I was ready.

We crested a sloping dune and saw the encampment beneath us. It stood in a small but lush oasis full of palms heavy with dates, surrounding a deep spring. These humans had two tents, both standing on the far side of the water. It was very late at night by now, and the oasis was silent except for the calls of owls and nightjars.

Nasr urged me forward with his legs. I understood that I was to move as silently as possible. The sand muffled my footsteps as I picked my way carefully down the far side of the dune. My ears were pricked toward the animals in the oasis. Most of them were sleeping, though a few horses and sheep were standing sentry over their herdmates. As we drew closer, one of the mares lifted her head to stare at us, though she didn't make a sound.

I was almost down the hill when I heard Zahrat coming up fast behind me. She was blowing each breath out through her nostrils with a little puffing sound, prancing as she went, despite Basim's efforts to soothe her.

Just then a dog barked. Zahrat's head shot up and she spurted forward.

No, I said to her through my body language, angling myself to block her from passing me. *We cannot panic. We must be quiet.*

Zahrat's head was still up. But her eyes were rolling toward me now, and her prancing hooves slowed. A second later, Basim was able to get her back under control.

Nasr gave me a pat, then steered me forward into the unfamiliar camp. All the animals were awakening by now, and one of the younger mares nickered curiously at our arrival. It was tempting to nicker back in the normal, friendly way of horses. But Nasr had trained me well, and I remained quiet. So did the others, even Zahrat.

"Go quickly," Nasr breathed to Basim. "Get a camel if you can. We'll follow shortly."

Basim nodded, then urged Zahrat forward.

For a moment, she danced in place, unwilling to comply. But I lowered my head toward her, doing my best to give her courage with my look. Finally she moved toward the camels.

I didn't see what she did after that, for Nasr turned me in the other direction. We rode in among the unfamiliar horses. They stared at me warily.

Then another dog barked. I felt Nasr's body tighten and understood that we had to act quickly.

Behind me, I could see Hasna and Ibtisam herding several sheep away from the others. Some of the creatures were letting out sleepy *baas* of protest, though they went where they were supposed to go.

It was easy to feel Nasr's every move when

he rode me, and now I felt his head turn to look toward the tents. Then he leaned over and grabbed the long flaxen mane of a fine-looking chestnut mare, quickly slipping a halter and rope onto her delicate head. He did the same to another horse, a half-grown dapple-gray filly.

Then he turned me with pressure from his legs, holding one lead rope in either hand while letting the reins fall upon my neck. That was fine with me; I needed nothing more to guide me.

We moved swiftly out of the camp, leading the two horses. The gray filly balked once, shaking her head and ready to call out in protest. But I could sense she was only feeling uncertain without her usual herd leader to guide her. I bumped her firmly with my body, throwing her off balance and earning a respectful look from

her. Nasr then gave a firm tug on the lead, and the filly followed along obediently.

Come, my beauty. It's time to go.

Nasr didn't speak the words aloud in the normal human way. But I understood him perfectly nonetheless. Turning toward the hilly dune, I trotted up its sandy slope. By now the other three war mares were at the top, along with the sheep and a gangly young camel.

Then—chaos. Several dogs came bursting toward us, barking for all they were worth. Seconds later, there came sleepy, confused shouts from the direction of the tents. A torch flared, the chestnut mare at my side let out a panicked whinny, and Nasr cursed under his breath.

"Let's go!" he shouted hoarsely, kicking me into a gallop.

I burst into motion, flying the rest of the way up the steep dune. Nasr kept hold of the two other horses, and they ran along beside me, though the younger one was not very fast.

We crested the top of the dune. Hasna, Zahrat, and Ibtisam were already well away with their charges, but I put my head down and raced swiftly after them, dragging the gray filly along. The chestnut mare was nearly as fast as I and seemed to be enjoying the run.

Where are you taking us? she asked me.

You shall see, I replied. *Now run as fast as you can!*

She let out a willing snort and dug in, almost passing me before I surged forward again. Before long we caught up to the others, who were hampered by the slower sheep.

"They're after us," Nasr called to his sons, slowing me to a canter beside them.

Basim looked over. "Should we take the horses and camel and leave the sheep behind?" he called.

"No. We need the sheep. Besides, that shouldn't be necessary." I felt Nasr glance over his shoulder.

With my greater range of vision, I could see that there was not yet anyone following us. But my sensitive ears could hear the nickers and dancing feet of horses being rapidly saddled and mounted, and I guessed that they would be upon us soon.

"Hasna is the swiftest horse in our group," Nasr said, pointing. "Fayyad, take her straight that way and see if you can draw their pursuit and keep them busy to allow us to get away. The rest of us will take the long route home."

Nasr's second-eldest son nodded and closed his legs on Hasna's sides, guiding the bay mare off to the left. Hasna obeyed for a stride or two. Then, seeing that the rest of us were not following but were in fact turning in the other direction, she began to resist, slowing to a stiff-legged, hopping gait and tossing her head high to escape the bridle.

Fayyad cursed, kicking firmly at the mare's sides as he tried to regain control. But Hasna's eyes were wide and anxious.

Do not leave me! she called to the rest of us in a panic. *I do not like to be alone!*

"Never mind," Nasr barked out. Spinning me around, he rode toward Hasna. "Here, you take these two. Yatimah and I will play the decoy instead."

Fayyad nodded, catching the lead ropes his father tossed his way. Then he turned Hasna and urged her on. For a second she hesitated, unwilling to part from me.

Go, I told her. *The others await you.*

Hasna saw Zahrat and Ibtisam and obeyed, cantering toward them with her ears pricked and the two strange mares following along. Soon they, along with the humans, sheep, and camel, were disappearing over the next rise.

"All right, my beauty," Nasr murmured, his hand briefly dropping to stroke my withers. "I wasn't expecting to test your speed and courage so soon, but I suppose this is as good a time as any."

He urged me on, away from the others. I felt

only the slightest moment of hesitation. Horses are meant to be in a herd, and it felt strange to rush away from them.

But Nasr was part of my herd, too, and he was still with me. I surged forward as he directed.

Moments later, cries rose behind us. Looking back, I saw several men on horseback crest the dune. Nasr let out a hoarse shout, momentarily slowing my speed as he glanced over his shoulder at the pursuers.

The other men shouted angrily in response, sending their horses after us. Nasr turned to face forward again, crouching down over my withers.

"Let's go, my beauty," he murmured.

He pressed me forward and I opened my stride, my legs pumping faster and faster as I flew over the sand. The other horses were fresher than

I, but I understood from my rider's urgency that we could not let them catch us, so I put every ounce of energy I had into staying ahead of them.

For about half an hour, we zigzagged among some craggy outcroppings. The other riders kept coming but couldn't quite catch up or even get a good look at us.

Finally we emerged into open desert. I charged forward, and Nasr once again looked back.

I was watching, too, as the other riders burst into view. The lead rider shouted out with annoyance. "There is only one horse ahead!" he cried. "It is a trick—the scoundrels have deceived us!"

"After him!" the next man exclaimed. "At least we can take his mare to make up for our losses this night!"

Nasr laughed out loud. "Praise to Allah, you shall never catch me while I ride this mare!" he shouted back.

He urged me on even faster, and I responded instantly. Of course I was tired after the long

night on the move, but I had been trained and conditioned well by Nasr and Basim, and had energy left still. The black night sky was also working in our favor, and despite our pursuers' best efforts, we finally left them behind us in the darkness.

Only then did my pace slow, first to a canter and then to a trot. "Well done, my fine mare," Nasr said, giving me a pat as his legs brought me at last to a walk. "You are every bit as fast and agile as your mother was, and equally bold. Thanks to you, we shall celebrate our spoils this night. Now let's go home."

Home was a word that I recognized, and I automatically turned toward our current oasis, for horses have a keen sense of direction. Indeed, Nasr allowed me to find my own way.

After a short rest at a walk, he allowed me to move into a ground-covering trot, one I could sustain for a long while without tiring too much.

By the time we neared the oasis, the pink fingers of dawn were on the horizon. Nasr slowed me again, and we drifted to a halt just outside the encampment.

The others were back already, though it was obvious they hadn't been there long—the women and children were still exclaiming over the new animals. The humans hadn't yet noticed our return, though Ibtisam lifted her head and glanced toward me. As a well-trained war mare, she did not call out, and neither did I, though I was eager to rejoin my herd as soon as Nasr allowed it. By tilting my head slightly, I could see him sitting upon my back with a smile on his face as he watched his family.

"Allah forgive me, my beauty," he murmured, stroking my neck without seeming to mind that it was damp with sweat after the long night of exertion. "You are not the same as your mother. But Sarab's blood runs in your veins. I should have trusted that you would be a fine horse in your own right."

I still didn't understand human language. But I knew Nasr well enough by now to be able to feel the sentiment behind his words. Despite my weariness, I arched my neck with pride.

"There they are!" a voice cried out.

It was Safiya. She had just spotted us in the growing light. Nasr chuckled, then urged me gently forward. I trotted into camp to join the others.

Safiya hurried forward to meet us. She waited for her father to dismount, then took hold of me by the bridle.

"I'll untack and groom her for you, Father," she offered.

"Thank you, daughter," Nasr replied, giving me one last pat. "Treat her well, for she has performed brilliantly this night. Yatimah is one of the two finest war mares I've ever had the pleasure to ride."

Safiya's eyes widened with surprise, and she looked at me with a proud smile. I lowered my head, blew a breath into her face, and then nuzzled her shoulder fondly.

Yes, I was a war mare now. And I was content with my ever-changing, ever-challenging life in the desert.

APPENDIX

MORE ABOUT THE ARABIAN HORSE

The Purest of Breeds

Arabians are thought to be the oldest breed of
horse in the world and also one of the purest,
their breeding dating back more than a thousand
years. They have often been used to create or

improve other breeds. Most common breeds of modern riding horses contain at least some Arabian blood in their background.

Arabian horses have always been bred for certain characteristics that make them stand out. They are instantly recognizable by their delicate, dished faces, their large eyes, and their high tail carriage.

Bedouin Treasures

Horses were a very important part of Bedouin life, sharing the Bedouins' nomadic lifestyle and harsh desert environment. Sometimes the Bedouins would even invite their horses into their tents to escape the weather. They also would feed them dates and camel's milk to

make up for the lack of grazing and water in the
desert. After countless generations of working so
closely with humans, Arabians are known for
their willing, friendly, and loyal temperament.
As an Arabian proverb says, "My treasures do

not clink together or glitter. They gleam in the sun and neigh in the night."

Although *Yatimah* takes place in the ninth century, the Bedouins lived much the same then as they did in the very early twentieth century, when the following photographs were taken.

The Bedouin Lifestyle

For hundreds of years, Bedouins lived a nomadic life, moving from place to place to subsist in the harsh deserts of northern Africa and the Middle East. They traveled in family units with a male leader, sheltered by tents that they could shift

easily as they moved to find water and grazing for their livestock. The Bedouins took great pride in their horse breeding and could recite their horses' lineage going back many generations, with emphasis on the great mare lines in the pedigree.

War Mares

The Bedouins preferred to ride mares rather than stallions, especially when going on raids. They believed that mares were less likely to call out to other horses during raids, when it was important to be as stealthy as possible. The Bedouin war mares were swift of foot, with great endurance, and could show great courage during battle. War mares were never for sale at any price, changing hands only through gift or theft.

Favorites of Many

Arabians have spread far beyond their original homelands. They are one of the most popular breeds in the world and were the chosen mount of a number of historical figures, including George Washington, Napoléon Bonaparte, and Ronald Reagan.

Unparalleled Endurance

Arabians are versatile horses and are used today in many different disciplines—trail riding, dressage, jumping, saddle seat, various Western events, and more. The sport in which Arabians are most dominant, however, is endurance racing,

in which horse and rider travel up to one hundred miles, often over challenging terrain. The Tevis Cup in California is one of the best-known endurance competitions. Since its first running in 1955, nearly all of the winners have been all or part Arabian.

COMING SOON!

California, 1935

Risky Chance is a gray Thoroughbred who was born to race. Life at the track, being spoiled by his jockey's young daughter, Marie, is all Chance could ask for. He loves nothing more than running fast and winning. But after an accident, he discovers a side of horse racing that has little to do with glory. Here is Risky Chance's story . . . in his own words.

About the Author

Catherine Hapka has written more than 150 books for children and young adults, including many about horses. A lifelong horse lover, she rides several times a week and appreciates horses of all breeds. In addition to writing and riding, she enjoys all kinds of animals, reading, gardening, music, and travel. She lives on a small farm in Chester County, Pennsylvania, which she shares with a horse, three goats, a small flock of chickens, and too many cats.

About the Illustrator

Ruth Sanderson grew up with a love for horses. She drew them constantly, and her first oil painting, at age fourteen, was a horse portrait.

Ruth has illustrated and retold many fairy tales and likes to feature horses in them whenever possible. Her book about a magical horse, *The Golden Mare, the Firebird, and the Magic Ring*, won the Texas Bluebonnet Award in 2003. She illustrated the first Black Stallion paperback covers and a number of chapter books about horses, most recently *Summer Pony* and *Winter Pony* by Jean Slaughter Doty.

Ruth and her daughter have two horses, an

Appaloosa named Thor and a quarter horse named Gabriel. She lives with her family in Massachusetts.

To find out more about her adventures with horses and the research she did to create the illustrations in this book, visit her website, ruthsanderson.com.

Collect all the books in the Horse Diaries series!

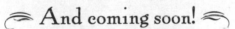

And coming soon!